D0573797

CALGARY PUBLIC LIBRARY

MAY   2019

A Special Gift
for Grammy

To Hunter and Sam
stone pile builders
—JEAN CRAIGHEAD GEORGE

In memory and honor of Jean Craighead George
— S.J. & L.F.

A Special Gift for Grammy
Text copyright © 2013 by Julie Productions, Inc.
Illustrations copyright © 2013 by Steve Johnson and Lou Fancher
All rights reserved. Manufactured in China.
No part of this book may be used or reproduced in any manner whatsoever without written permission except in the case of brief quotations embodied in critical articles and reviews. For information address HarperCollins Children's Books, a division of HarperCollins Publishers, 10 East 53rd Street, New York, NY 10022.
www.harpercollinschildrens.com

Library of Congress Cataloging-in-Publication Data
George, Jean Craighead, date
    A special gift for Grammy / Jean Craighead George ; illustrations by Steve Johnson and Lou Fancher.— 1st ed.
        p.   cm.
    Summary: When Hunter collects a pile of stones that he leaves on his grandmother's porch, they are used by the neighbors for a myriad of purposes—and by Hunter to make a special necklace for his grammy.
    ISBN 978-0-06-053176-8
    [1. Rocks—Fiction.   2. Grandmothers—Fiction.]   I. Johnson, Steve, date, ill.   II. Fancher, Lou, ill.   III. Title.
PZ7.G2933Sp   2013   2011030450
[E]—dc23   CIP
                                                                                                                                      AC

Book Design by Lou Fancher
The artists used collage, acrylic, and pencil on Strathmore Series 500 3-ply paper to create the illustrations for this book.
13 14 15 16 17 SCP 10 9 8 7 6 5 4 3 2 1

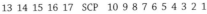

First Edition

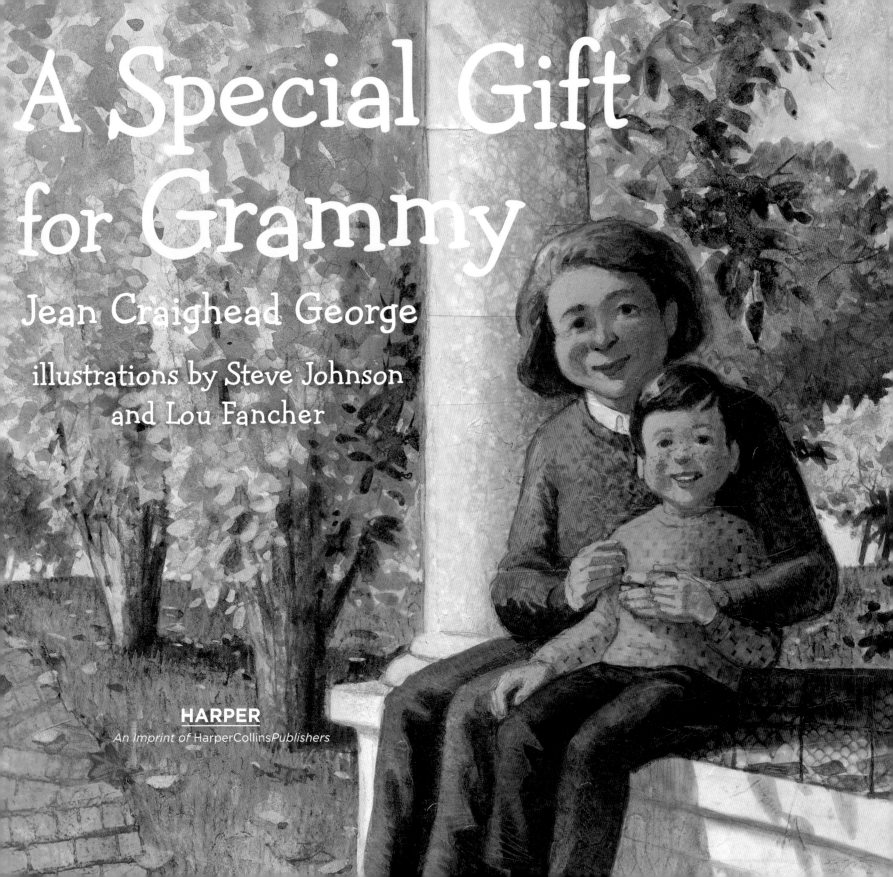

A Special Gift
for Grammy

Jean Craighead George

illustrations by Steve Johnson
and Lou Fancher

HARPER

An Imprint of HarperCollinsPublishers

Hunter picked up a stone.

He put it on his grammy's porch.

He went back to the road for another stone,
and another and another.

By suppertime he had a pile of stones, big and small.

"What are the stones for?" his dad asked.

"For Grammy," Hunter said.

"What will she do with a pile of stones?"

"What everyone does with a pile of stones."

"Oh, yes," said Dad.

As Grammy kissed Hunter good-bye, she saw the pile of stones.

"What do I do with a pile of stones?" she asked Hunter.

"What everyone does with a pile of stones," he answered.

"Of course," said Grammy.

The stones sat quietly all night and all the next day,
and the next day and the next.

On Monday the mail carrier saw the stone pile.

She picked up the largest stone and put it on
the letters so the wind would not blow them away.

"Of course," said Grammy.

A neighbor came to Grammy's house to borrow some sugar. She saw the pile of stones and picked up two.

She said, "I will place them on the graves of my favorite dog and cat."

"Of course," said Grammy.

A Brownie came to Grammy's house to deliver cookies.
She took three stones from the stone pile. She stacked them
on the sidewalk so that her friends would know to turn right.
"Of course," said the Brownies, and turned right.

The carpenter tied a stone to a plumb line. He measured the tilt of Grammy's screen door and fixed it.

"Of course," said Grammy.

Grammy's sister took a basket of stones to mark off her rose bed.

The gardener hammered a stake with a stone.

A boy put a stone in front of each wheel of his wagon to keep it from rolling downhill.

When Hunter came back to visit Grammy, only six small stones were left.

Hunter said, "See? Everyone knew what to do with a stone pile."

He scratched his head. Then he rubbed his chin. "What do I do with a pile of six little stones?"

Hunter stared at the stones for a long time.
Finally he picked one up. He turned it over.

"Grammy," he called, "come see what I see!"

Grammy came out on the porch. "What do you see?"
she asked.

"This stone is my baby shoe," he said, handing it to her.
She held it carefully.

Hunter picked up another stone.

"This one is my rubber duck." He gave it to Grammy.

"And this one is my comfy pillow." Grammy held out her hand.

He picked up a fourth stone and turned it over and upside down
and over again.

"It's my rocking horse," he said, and gave it to Grammy.

Hunter picked up the fifth stone. It was flat.

"I don't know what this is," he said.

He put it in his pocket, then picked up the sixth stone. It was round and bumpy, with two dents like eyes. He stared and stared.

"This one is me!" Hunter said in surprise.

Grammy looked at the stones too.

"Of course," said Grammy.

Hunter frowned. "What do we do with five Hunter stones?" he asked.

"I know," Grammy said. She took Hunter's hand.

They walked to the stonecutter's workshop.

"Please drill a little hole in this baby-shoe stone," Grammy said. "And in this rubber-duck stone, the comfy-pillow stone, the rocking-horse stone, and last, a hole in the Hunter stone."

Grammy and Hunter waited.

Hunter took the stone he had saved out of his pocket. He turned it over and over.

"Why don't you show that stone to the stonecutter?" Grammy said. "Maybe he'll see what it is."

"I know what it is," said Hunter.

He put it back in his pocket.

When the stonecutter had drilled a hole in each stone, Grammy threaded a leather cord through them.

"It's a grandmother necklace!" exclaimed Hunter.

"Of course," said Grammy. She put it on.

Hunter and Grammy walked home.

When they came to the lake, Hunter stopped.

He took the stone out of his pocket.

He leaned to his right and threw it.

The stone skipped lightly over the water,

made four bright growing circles, and sank.

"It's a skipping stone," said Hunter.

"Of course," Grammy said, and smiled.

"We all know what to do with a pile of stones."